Sojourn®
THE WARRIOR'S
TALE

D1065849

Publisher s Cataloging-in-Publication Data
(Prepared by The Donohue Group, Inc.)

Sojourn. Volume three : the warrior s tale / Writer: Ron Marz ; Penciler: Greg Land ; Inker: Jay Leisten ; Colorist: Justin Ponsor.

p. : ill. ; cm.

Spine title: Sojourn. 3 : the warrior s tale

ISBN: 1-931484-65-1

1. Fantasy fiction. 2. Graphic novels. 3. Mordath (Fictitious character) Fiction. 4. Arwyn (Fictitious character) Fiction. 5. Gareth (Fictitious character) Fiction. 6. Bohr (Fictitious character) Fiction. 7. Ankhara (Imaginary place) Fiction. I. Marz, Ron. II. Land, Greg. III. Leisten, Jay. IV. Ponsor, Justin. V. Title: Warrior s tale VI. Title: Sojourn. 3 : the warrior s tale.

PN6728 .S65 2003
813.54 [Fic]

THE WARRIOR'S TALE

Ron MARZ
WRITER

Greg LAND
PENCILER

Jay LEISTEN
INKER

Justin PONSOR
COLORIST

Troy PETERI · LETTERER

CHAPTER 13
Caesar RODRIGUEZ · COLORIST

CHAPTER 17
Aaron LOPRESTI · PENCILER
Roland PARIS · INKER
Laura MARTIN · COLORIST

CrossGeneration Comics
Oldsmar, Florida

The Warrior's Tale

features Chapters 13-18
of the ongoing series
SOJOURN

The Quest

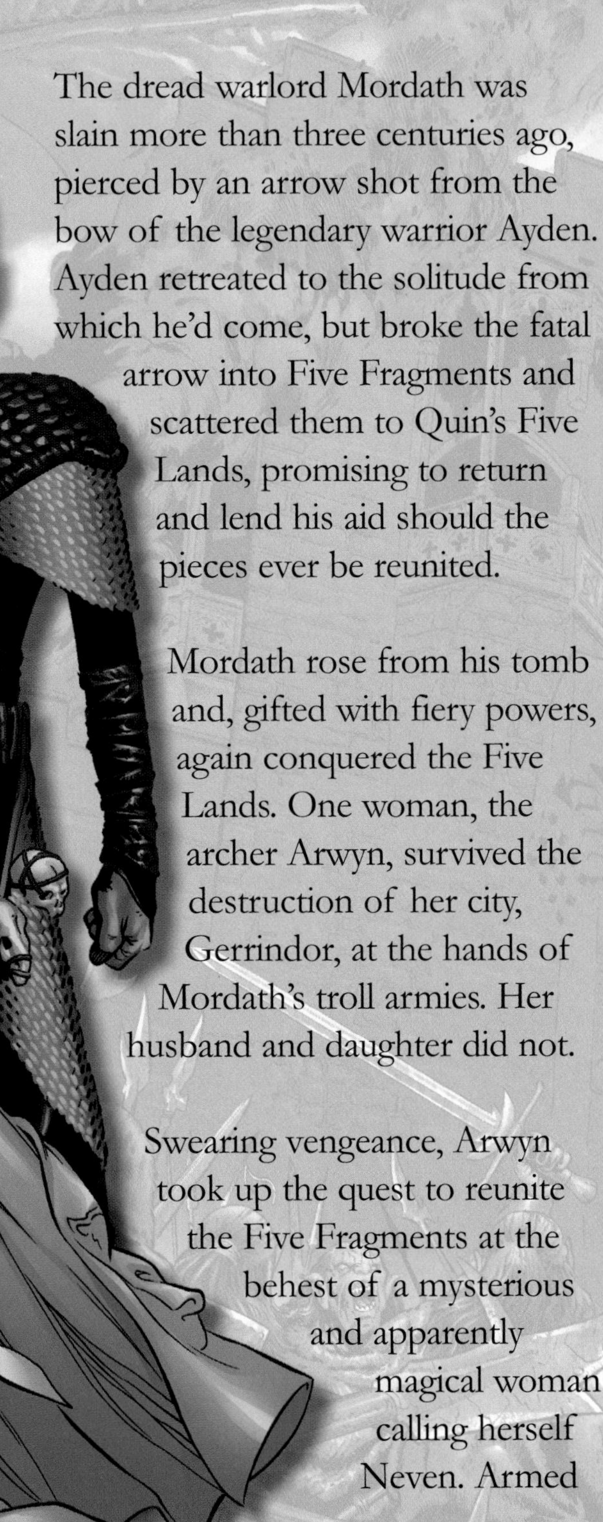

The dread warlord Mordath was slain more than three centuries ago, pierced by an arrow shot from the bow of the legendary warrior Ayden. Ayden retreated to the solitude from which he'd come, but broke the fatal arrow into Five Fragments and scattered them to Quin's Five Lands, promising to return and lend his aid should the pieces ever be reunited.

Mordath rose from his tomb and, gifted with fiery powers, again conquered the Five Lands. One woman, the archer Arwyn, survived the destruction of her city, Gerrindor, at the hands of Mordath's troll armies. Her husband and daughter did not.

Swearing vengeance, Arwyn took up the quest to reunite the Five Fragments at the behest of a mysterious and apparently magical woman calling herself Neven. Armed

Thus Far

with Ayden's bow and accompanied by the adventurer Gareth and her dog Kreeg, Arwyn dedicated herself to bringing about Mordath's destruction.

Arwyn found the first fragment in Middelyn, obtaining it from the treasure hoard of a shape-changing dragon. The dragon, Shiara, was slain in an unsuccessful attack on Mordath's keep. Though Arwyn and Gareth narrowly escaped, Shiara's death added to the weight of Arwyn's guilt.

Arwyn then turned south toward the cliffs of Ankhara as a detachment of troll pursuers, led by Captain Bohr of Mordath's guard, picked up her trail.

LAND
GERACI
CÆSAR

I TOLD THEM I DIDN'T HAVE TIME FOR THIS.

FOOLS...

...YOUR PETTY THIEVERY LOST ME TOO MUCH TIME, AND THE WEATHER'S GOING TO *WORSEN*.

HERE, HORSE.

LET'S SEE HOW MUCH GROUND WE CAN COVER BEFORE THE STORM CLOSES IN. MY *HOME* CALLS ME...

...AND EVERY MOMENT I'M AWAY ONLY *ADDS* TO THE SUFFERING.

KRAKOOM

HO!
STEADY, YOU MISERABLE BEAST!

WE CAN FIGHT THIS GALE NO LONGER, HORSE.
WE'LL TAKE SHELTER UNTIL THE WORST OF THE STORM PASSES.

UNDER THERE.

AT LEAST WE'LL BE DRY.
COME ALONG, HORSE.
YOUR OTHER CHOICE IS TO STAY OUT THERE AND BE SOAKED.
WHAT'S GOT YOU SO SPOOKED?
SOMETHING YOU DON'T LIKE?
SOMETHING DEEPER IN THE CAVE.

HRROOWL

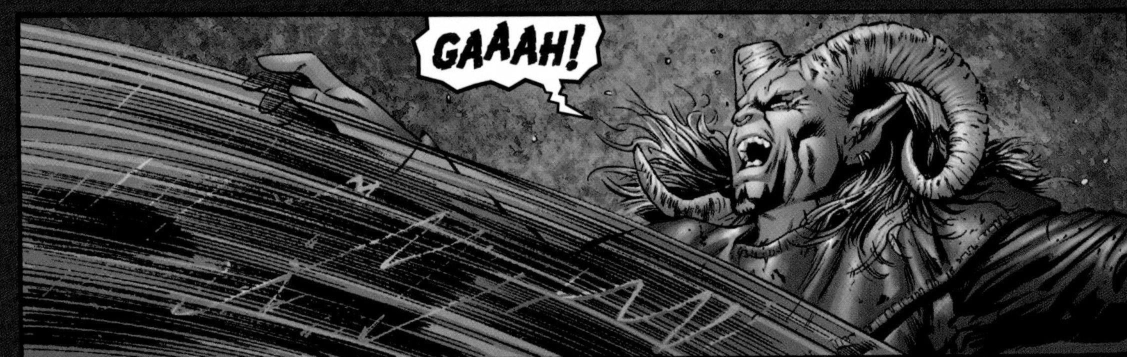
GAAAH!

GRRROW

ARRRAR
SHLUK

HWNF!
HRROOWL
COME, BEAST!
CHUKT
LET US END THIS...
...THIS...

PROTECTING YOUR CUBS. WHAT ANY MOTHER WOULD DO.
THEN WE UNDERSTAND EACH OTHER...

...DON'T WE?
I'LL LEAVE YOU IN PEACE...

...YOU DO THE SAME FOR ME.

THIS IS NO PLACE FOR *US,* HORSE.
BETTER WE FACE THE *STORM*...
...THAN A *MOTHER* PROTECTING HER OWN.

A RIDER!

RAISE THE GATES!
A RIDER APPROACHES!

BOHR.
IT'S GOOD TO HAVE YOU HOME AGAIN. YOU'VE BEEN TOO LONG ABSENT FROM THIS PLACE.

SHE WAITS FOR YOU.
IT IS... FORTUNATE... THAT YOU CAME WHEN YOU DID.
WOULD THAT I HAD BEEN ABLE TO ARRIVE SOONER, OLD FRIEND.
MY DUTIES FOR LORD MORDATH HAD TAKEN ME FAR FROM GRINBOR'S FORESTS.

MY MOUNT'S BEEN RIDDEN LONG AND HARD, GNARN. CAN YOU SEE TO IT?
OF COURSE, BOHR.
THIS IS NOT THE HOMECOMING I DESIRED...

...BUT AT LEAST I HAVE WHAT SHE NEEDS.

I HOPE THE RELIEF I BRING DOES NOT COME TOO LATE.
I DON'T KNOW WHICH WILL BE SWEETER TO HER, BOHR. WHAT YOU BRING...
...OR MERELY SEEING HER SON'S FACE AGAIN.

GRENNA.
YOU'RE HERE.
FINALLY.

I CAME AS QUICKLY AS I COULD ONCE WORD REACHED ME, SISTER.
I LEFT MY COMMAND WITHOUT PERMISSION. THERE WILL BE HELL TO PAY IF WORD EVER REACHES MORDATH'S FORTRESS...
...BUT THE MEN WHO RIDE BEHIND ME ARE LOYAL. I CAN TRUST THEM.

HOW IS SHE?
NOT GOOD, AND GROWING WORSE.
SHE'S BEEN ASKING FOR YOU.

YOU BROUGHT IT?
YES.

THEN GO TO HER.
SHE'S WAITED LONG ENOUGH.

MOTHER...

...I'M HERE.
MY SON?
YOU CAME.
I'M SORRY.
I'M SORRY. I WOULD HAVE BEEN HERE SOONER, BUT...

Shhh
NO APOLOGIES.
YOU HAVE YOUR DUTIES. YOU SERVE A GLORIOUS LORD WHO HAS RAISED OUR PEOPLE TO GREATNESS IN THE FIVE LANDS.
BUT OUR HOUSE IS *BETTER* FOR YOUR PRESENCE WITHIN ITS WALLS AGAIN.

GRENNA SAYS THE PAIN IS BAD.
I HAVE NOT THE STRENGTH TO LIE TO YOU, BOHR.
THE WASTING EATS AWAY AT ME. SOON THERE WILL BE NOTHING LEFT SAVE A SHELL.
FORTUNE SMILED UPON YOUR FATHER WHEN IT GAVE HIM A *BATTLEFIELD DEATH,* RATHER THAN THIS.

BUT YOU BRING ME *MERCY*, DON'T YOU?
I...
...YES. I HAVE IT HERE.

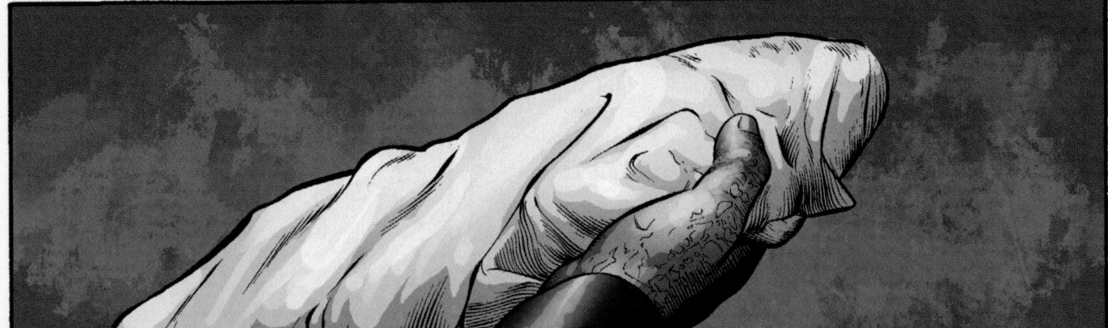

THAT BLADE HAS BEEN IN OUR CLAN FOR GENERATIONS, PASSED TO EACH ELDEST CHILD.
IT'S BEAUTIFUL, ISN'T IT?

YES.

MY SWEET SON.
IT HAS *ALWAYS* BEEN THIS WAY IN THE CLANS. IT FALLS TO THE ELDEST TO END THE SUFFERING OF THOSE WITHOUT HOPE.
WE DELIVER THE SAME MERCY TO A HORSE WITH A SHATTERED LEG, OR A SICKLY STEER. WHY WOULD WE NOT DO SO FOR THOSE WE LOVE?

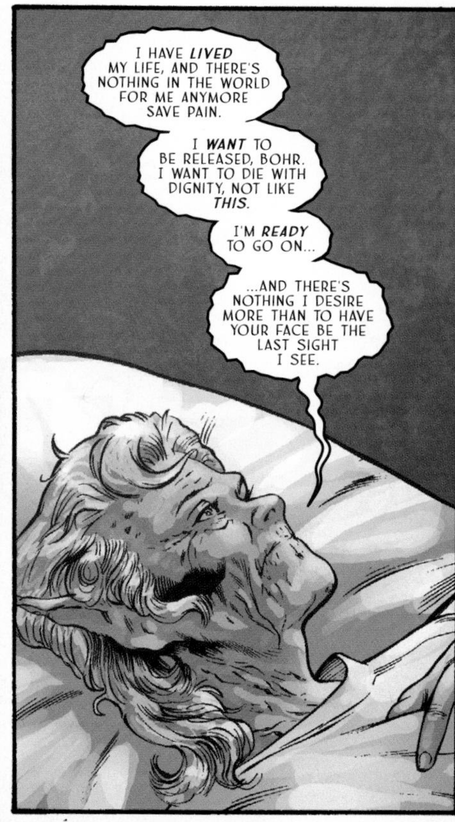
I HAVE *LIVED* MY LIFE, AND THERE'S NOTHING IN THE WORLD FOR ME ANYMORE SAVE PAIN.
I *WANT* TO BE RELEASED, BOHR. I WANT TO DIE WITH DIGNITY, NOT LIKE *THIS*.
I'M *READY* TO GO ON...
...AND THERE'S NOTHING I DESIRE MORE THAN TO HAVE YOUR FACE BE THE LAST SIGHT I SEE.

I REMEMBER WHEN I WAS A BOY, JUST A SMALL CHILD, AND THE STORMS WOULD COME AT NIGHT.
THE HOUSE WOULD BE DARK, AND THE RAIN WOULD HAMMER THE WINDOWS. THE WIND WOULD SHAKE THE HOUSE.
FATHER WAS AWAY TO THE CLAN WARS. I WAS *AFRAID,* BUT I WOULD COME HERE AND CLIMB INTO THIS BED WITH YOU.
AND YOU WOULD MAKE ME FEEL *SAFE.*

MOTHER, I...
...I...
MY BEAUTIFUL, PROUD SON.
AFTER ALL THESE YEARS, THERE'S NO NEED FOR WORDS. NOT ANYMORE.
I RAISED YOU TO BE STRONG. BE STRONG ENOUGH TO GRANT ME THIS.

IT'S DONE.
I FEEL **RELIEVED.** SHOULD I BE **ASHAMED** TO FEEL THAT WAY?
I DON'T KNOW HOW YOU BROUGHT YOURSELF TO DO IT, BOHR. I DON'T KNOW HOW YOU—
IT WAS WHAT SHE WANTED.
IT WAS **RIGHT.**
YOU'LL SEE TO HER BODY?
I WILL.
YOU CAN'T STAY, BROTHER?
NO.
I'VE SEEN TO MY DUTY HERE...
...NOW THE DUTY TO MY **COMMAND** BECKONS ME, GRENNA.
MY LORD MORDATH CHARGED ME WITH HUNTING DOWN A THREAT TO HIM, AN **ARCHER,** AND I DARE NOT FAIL HIM.
MY QUARRY JOURNEYS SOUTH...

"...AND SO MUST I."
THIS FAR SOUTH? YOU THINK THEY'RE *STILL* AFTER US?

THOSE TROLLS HAVE A BETTER NOSE FOR A TRAIL THAN THIS *DOG* OF YOURS, ARWYN.
THEY MIGHT EVEN BE A FEW *DAYS* BEHIND US...

...BUT THEY'RE BACK THERE. AND THEY WON'T GIVE UP.
SO WHAT ARE YOU SAYING, GARETH? WE SHOULD EXPECT THEM TO FOLLOW US ALL THE WAY INTO ANKHARA?
AND *BEYOND*. BUT I'M TRUTHFULLY MORE CONCERNED ABOUT *US*.
THE HARD PART ISN'T GETTING *TO* ANKHARA...

...IT'S GETTING *INTO* ANKHARA.

LAND
GERACI
CÆSAR

Once, they were magnificent.

They soared above their homeland like great, graceful birds of prey basking in the sun's radiance.
At one time their civilization was perhaps the pinnacle of the Five Lands.

Their cities, hewn from the cliffs, were centers of art and learning in times of peace, impregnable strongholds in times of war.
The Ankharans were a hard people to know, suspicious as they were of outsiders, of those of us who were bound to earth.
Whenever I traveled in their lands, I was always a visitor, never a guest.
But I suppose none of that much matters now.
When Mordath the Undead led his troll armies across the Five Lands, conquering each in turn, Ankhara fell like all the others, painted in blood and fire.
The trolls occupied every Ankharan city, including this – Ankhara itself, the seat of power.
Its natives became little better than slaves in their own aeries, while the trolls turn their sacred places into foul pits.

So our plan of action...
THUK
...naturally...
THUK
...was to walk right into the middle of it all.
THUK

Hmf.
DRIFTING TO THE RIGHT A LITTLE.

I DON'T LIKE THIS SITTING AND *WAITING,* GARETH.
NEITHER DO I...
...BUT IT'S BETTER THAN GETTING ANXIOUS AND DOING SOMETHING ***STUPID*** SO THE TROLLS HAVE A CHANCE TO GRAB US UP.
WE'D BE PRETTY SEVERELY OUTNUMBERED EVEN IF YOU ***WEREN'T*** NURSING THAT ARM, ARWYN.

THE WAY IT'S FEELING IT'LL BE AT LEAST ANOTHER ***WEEK*** BEFORE I CAN THINK ABOUT GETTING RID OF THIS SLING.
AND I DON'T KNOW ***HOW LONG*** BEFORE I'LL BE ABLE TO PULL A BOW AGAIN.

YEAH, WELL, AT LEAST ***ONE*** OF US HAD BETTER BE ABLE TO SHOOT STRAIGHT. THIS PLACE IS ***LOUSY*** WITH TROLLS.
ALL THE MORE REASON I WANT TO GET IN AND GET OUT BEFORE ANY OF THEM EVEN KNOW WE'RE HERE.

AND HOW DO WE GET INTO ANKHARA? YOU'VE BEEN A LITTLE TIGHT-LIPPED ABOUT THAT PART.
PATIENCE, MY GOLDEN-TRESSED SIDEKICK.
I THOUGHT YOU WERE MY ONE-EYED SIDEKICK.

THE ANKHARANS USED THE CLIFFS AS NATURAL BARRIERS WHEN THEY BUILT THEIR CITIES. THEY SEALED ANY GAPS AND CONSTRUCTED GATES.
THE CLIFFS ARE TOO SHEER TO EVEN THINK ABOUT SCALING THEM. PRETTY EFFECTIVE DETERRENT IF YOU DON'T HAVE WINGS.
THOUGH EVEN THAT WASN'T ENOUGH TO KEEP OUT MORDATH'S LEGIONS.
SO YOU'RE SAYING WE'VE GOT NO CHOICE BUT TO GO THROUGH THE GATES? YOU THINK YOU CAN TAKE THE GUARDS FROM UP THERE?
IF I COULD GET CLOSER...

"...COMPENSATE FOR THE WIND, SHOOT QUICKLY ENOUGH TO TAKE THEM ALL, MAYBE. BUT THERE'S PLENTY MORE INSIDE..."

...AND KILLING ONE IS THE SUREST WAY TO ALERT THE OTHERS.
SO WE'RE BACK TO HOW WE GET IN.
NOT TO WORRY. I'VE GOT A PLAN...

"...BUT WE HAVE TO WAIT UNTIL *NIGHTFALL*."
IT'S JUST UP THERE, PAST THE—
DAMN.
AHH, THAT *SWILL* THE ANKHARANS BREW AS BEER GOES RIGHT THROUGH YOU.
TRUE ENOUGH...
...BUT IT'S THE ONLY THING MAKING GUARD DUTY TOLERABLE.
GRR
WHAT WAS *THAT*?
I THOUGHT I HEARD SOMETHING. A *SOUND*.
GRRR

SEE? THERE IT WAS AGAIN.
BUT I DON'T—
STAND STILL AND *LISTEN*.

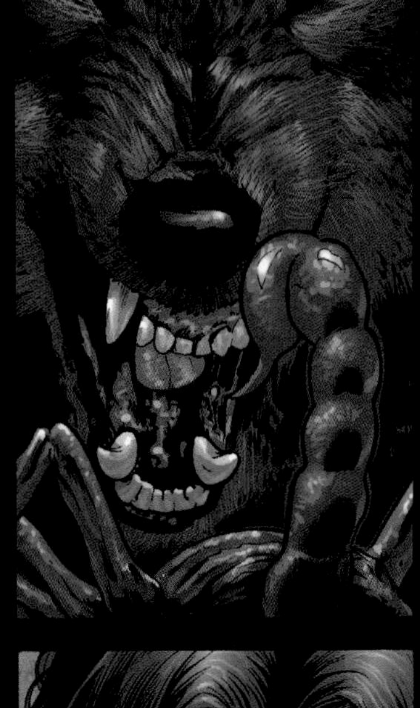

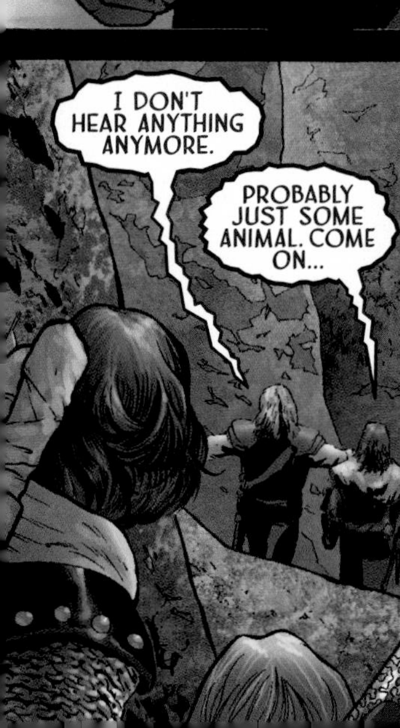
I DON'T HEAR ANYTHING ANYMORE.
PROBABLY JUST SOME ANIMAL. COME ON...

...WE SHOULD GET BACK BEFORE WE'RE MISSED.

THIS WAY.

HANG ON...
...GIVE ME A MOMENT FOR THIS TO CATCH...
...*THERE*.

GARETH, WHAT *IS* THIS PLACE?
THE CLIFFS ARE *HONEYCOMBED* WITH TUNNELS BUILT BY THE ANKHARANS. A FEW OF THEM TERMINATE IN HIDDEN ENTRANCES OUTSIDE THE CLIFFS, LIKE THE ONE WE USED TO GET IN HERE.
THESE PASSAGEWAYS REACH PLACES ALL OVER THE CITY. I'VE NEEDED TO USE THEM ONCE OR TWICE BEFORE WHEN I WAS IN ANKHARA.
THE TUNNELS ARE WELL-DISGUISED.
I DOUBT VERY MUCH THE TROLLS ARE CURIOUS ENOUGH TO HAVE DISCOVERED THEM.

AND WHAT'S THIS ON THE WALLS?
IT'S BEAUTIFUL.

HERE.
THAT'S THE ANKHARAN FORM OF WRITING. I CAN'T BEGIN TO TELL YOU WHAT IT SAYS, BUT I KNOW THEY'RE BIG ON HISTORY AND ANCESTORS.

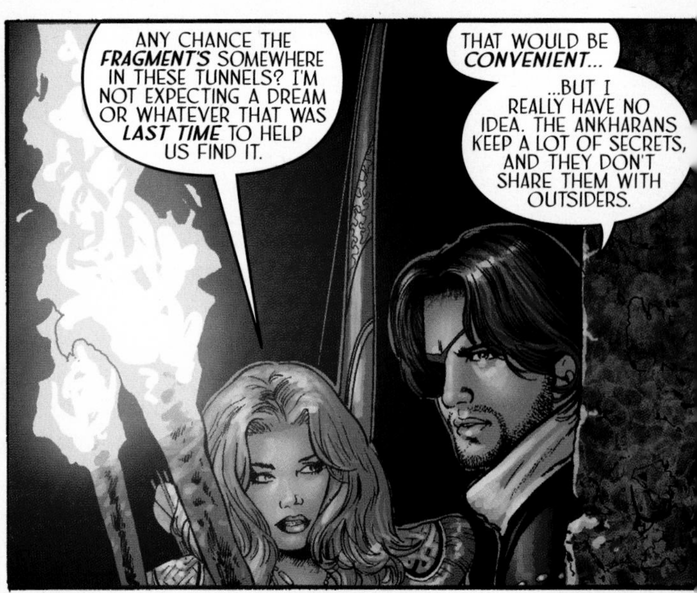
ANY CHANCE THE FRAGMENT'S SOMEWHERE IN THESE TUNNELS? I'M NOT EXPECTING A DREAM OR WHATEVER THAT WAS LAST TIME TO HELP US FIND IT.
THAT WOULD BE CONVENIENT...
...BUT I REALLY HAVE NO IDEA. THE ANKHARANS KEEP A LOT OF SECRETS, AND THEY DON'T SHARE THEM WITH OUTSIDERS.

BUT YOU AT LEAST KNOW YOUR WAY AROUND IN HERE?
ABSOLUTELY.
THIS IS THE WAY WE NEED TO...

...uh...
...WAIT, I THINK MAYBE IT'S THIS DIRECTION...
...um...
YOU REALLY DON'T KNOW WHERE YOU'RE GOING, DO YOU?
OF COURSE I KNOW WHERE I'M...
...WELL, YOU KNOW, I JUST NEED A MINUTE TO REMEMBER WHICH PASSAGE IS...

Oh, FOR AYDEN'S SAKE...

...JUST *PICK* ONE.

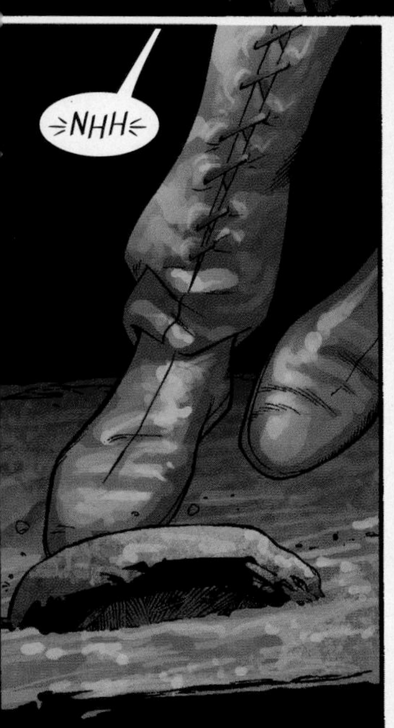
NHH

OUCH.
NOT EXACTLY THE MOST GRACEFUL ENTRANCE I'VE EVER—

AHH!

A PLACE OF THE *DEAD*...
...THIS IS A PLACE OF THE DEAD...
...THIS IS A...

DON'T SCREAM AGAIN...
MMPH

I WASN'T GOING TO. IT JUST STARTLED ME, THAT'S ALL.
WHAT KIND OF PLACE IS THIS?
YOU WERE RIGHT THE FIRST TIME. IT'S A PLACE OF THE DEAD.
THIS IS ONE OF THEIR BURIAL CHAMBERS. THE ANKHARANS MUMMIFY THEIR DEAD, AT LEAST THE IMPORTANT ONES...

...AND THEN PUT THEM IN TOMBS LIKE THIS.
THEY BELIEVE THE DEAD HAVE TO BE PREPARED FOR AN AFTERLIFE. THERE'S A WHOLE CEREMONY INVOLVED, VERY MYSTICAL STUFF, I GUESS.
THE CLIFFS ARE RIDDLED WITH THESE CHAMBERS.

LOVELY.
BY THE WAY, ARE YOU ALL RIGHT? THAT WAS A HARD TUMBLE.
DIDN'T HURT YOUR ARM AGAIN, DID YOU?
I'M NO WORSE FOR THE EXPERIENCE.
SNFF SNFF

LET'S *GO,* KREEG.
COME ON, I'VE GOT MY *BEARINGS* AGAIN.

I DON'T THINK WE'RE FAR NOW. JUST A BIT FURTHER THIS WAY...

...AND WE'LL BE ABLE TO GET INTO THE CITY WITHOUT EVEN BEING *SEEN*.

THAT'S IT.

THAT'S WHAT? ARE YOU SURE YOU KNOW WHERE YOU'RE GOING, GARETH?
IT LOOKS LIKE A BLANK WALL.
LOOKS LIKE.
SEE THE CRACK HERE? IT'S HINGED.
THE OTHER SIDE LETS OUT INTO THE BACK OF AN ALLEY. WE'LL NEVER BE NOTICED.

THERE'S A LITTLE CATCH ALONG HERE, AND ONCE YOU'VE FOUND THAT...
NNF
...YOU JUST PUSH.
THAT'S GOT IT.

WELL?
ARE WE IN THE RIGHT SPOT?
YEAH...

...YEAH, I THINK YOU COULD SAY THAT.

LADIES.

GARETH?
GARETH, EXACTLY WHAT SORT OF DESERTED ALLEY IS THIS?
SO MY SENSE OF DIRECTION IS A LITTLE IMPAIRED. BUT REALLY...
...WHO'S COMPLAINING?

WHO ARE YOU?
WHAT ARE YOU DOING IN THE GOVERNOR'S HAREM CHAMBERS?
DID THE DAWN WARRIOR SEND YOU?

DAWN WARRIOR? I DON'T KNOW ANY—
AWAKE, YOU HARRIDANS!
THE GUARDS ARE COMING!

ARWYN!
ARWYN, GET OUT OF—

YOU THERE!

HE WANTS THREE OF THEM FOR LATER.
UNCHAIN THOSE TWO AND THE NEW ONE.
YOU.
WHERE DID YOU COME FROM?

I CAN NEVER TELL YOUR KIND APART, BUT I ONLY EVER REMEMBER ONE HUMAN FEMALE IN HERE...
...AND YOU'RE NOT HER. SHE DIDN'T HAVE HER ARM IN THAT THING.
STILL...

...I SUPPOSE YOU'LL DO.
YOU'RE NOT AS UGLY AS MOST HUMANS.

KREEG, MY FRIEND, *THIS* ISN'T GOING TO END WELL.

GAAHG!

"LET'S NOT DRAW ATTENTION TO OURSELVES, ARWYN."
"LET'S GET IN AND OUT BEFORE THE TROLLS EVER KNOW WE'RE THERE, ARWYN."
THAT REALLY SUNK IN, DIDN'T IT?
RRARF

THE GOVERNOR CAN PICK ANOTHER FOR HIS NIGHT'S PLEASURE...
...YOU'RE GOING TO BE DEAD!

URGF!

I DON'T NEED TWO ARMS FOR THE LIKES OF YOU.

WHERE DID YOU COME FROM, HUMAN?
YOU MEAN JUST NOW...
NHN
...OR WERE YOU ASKING ABOUT MY MOTHER?

AAGH!

GHRK!

GHLLLK

ARWYN!
CAN I HAVE A WORD?
GHG!

WHAT HAPPENED TO US NOT CAUSING A DISTURBANCE? DO YOU REMEMBER THAT CONVERSATION, OR DID I JUST—

HRK!
TELL ME WHO YOU ARE...

...AND THEN TELL ME WHY I SHOULDN'T *KILL YOU*.

LAND
LEISTEN
CÆSAR

OPEN THE GATES.

Hnnff
Mnff

WAKE UP, YOU MISERABLE CUR!
UWFF?!

I AM BOHR, CAPTAIN OF OUR LORD MORDATH'S GUARD.
I AM NOT BLESSED WITH GREAT PATIENCE.
BUT, AS IT SEEMS YOUR MOTHER MUST HAVE DROPPED YOU ON YOUR HEAD AS AN INFANT, I'LL REPEAT MYSELF.

OPEN THE GATES.

MY MEN AND I SEEK TWO HUMANS JOURNEYING TOWARD ANKHARA.
THEY MAY WELL BE WITHIN THE CITY ALREADY.

BUT...THAT WOULD BE IMPOSSIBLE, SIR. NO ONE HAS ENTERED HERE.
NO ONE.

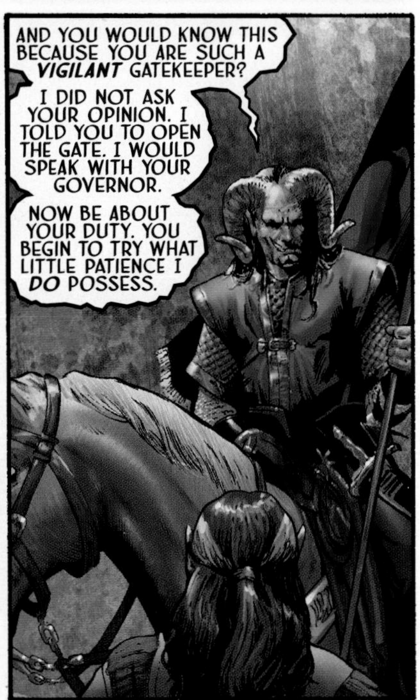
AND YOU WOULD KNOW THIS BECAUSE YOU ARE SUCH A VIGILANT GATEKEEPER?
I DID NOT ASK YOUR OPINION. I TOLD YOU TO OPEN THE GATE. I WOULD SPEAK WITH YOUR GOVERNOR.
NOW BE ABOUT YOUR DUTY. YOU BEGIN TO TRY WHAT LITTLE PATIENCE I DO POSSESS.

AND BE AWARE THAT GUARDS CAUGHT SLEEPING ON DUTY IN *MORDATH'S* FORTRESS ARE PUT TO THE TORCH.
YES, SIR!

OPEN THE GATES!
OPEN THE GATES!

CAPTAIN?
YOU TRULY BELIEVE OUR PREY HAS ALREADY ENTERED ANKHARA?
THEY WERE RESOURCEFUL ENOUGH TO GAIN ENTRANCE TO MORDATH'S FORTRESS.
TWICE.
AND THEY'VE ALWAYS MANAGED TO STAY JUST AHEAD OF OUR REACH.

I WOULD ONLY BE SURPRISED IF THEY HAD ***NOT*** DISCOVERED SOME WAY TO PASS INTO ANKHARA UNDETECTED.
BUT WE'LL FIND THEM. AND WHEN WE DO...

"...***THIS TIME*** THEY WON'T SLIP THROUGH OUR GRASP."

Grip like a vise.
GHHHP
HHKK
KHH

Which is about what you'd expect from a guy a good two heads taller than me.
With wings.
DO YOU KNOW WHAT YOU'VE *DONE?*
DO YOU?!

And a thick skull.
ANGH!

To be fair, I've met some very nice people who were initially trying to throttle the life out of me.
At least one of them was in a harem, too.
So, no, our introduction to the Ankharan resistance wasn't quite the sort of heroic tale they tell around campfires.
Certainly wasn't the first time I'd gotten into a little trouble when there was a woman involved. Or the last. Or even one of the more serious ones.
Come to think of it, that's how I got tangled up in this whole quest to begin with.
Because of **her.**
WE ARE ***NOT*** YOUR ENEMIES.
NO?
THEN WHAT ***SHOULD*** I CALL YOU...
KAFF
KAFF

...WHEN YOU DESTROYED A PLOT WE SO CAREFULLY SET INTO MOTION?
STOP IT, RAHM!
I BELIEVE SHE SPEAKS THE TRUTH.
TIYE?
THEY ARRIVED THROUGH THE TUNNELS.
WHEN THE TROLLS CAME TO TAKE US...
...THEY SLEW THEM.
I DON'T BELIEVE THEY'RE ENEMIES.
BUT I ALSO DON'T KNOW WHO THEY ARE OR WHY THEY'RE HERE.

MY NAME IS ARWYN.
THIS IS GARETH...
...THAT'S MY DOG, KREEG.
I HAIL FROM MIDDELYN. GARETH'S FROM...EVERYWHERE. WE MEANT NO HARM.
SO MAYBE YOU SHOULD BE A LITTLE MORE CAREFUL ABOUT WHO YOU'RE CHOKING.
LOOKED LIKE THERE WAS A PRETTY HORRIBLE FATE IN THE LADIES' IMMEDIATE FUTURE, SO WE TRIED TO SAVE THEM FROM IT.
AT LEAST THAT'S HOW IT TURNED OUT.
THEY DIDN'T NEED SAVING.
THESE WOMEN ALLOWED THEMSELVES TO BE CAPTURED FOR THE HAREM IN ORDER TO GET CLOSE ENOUGH TO THIS NEW GOVERNOR TO ASSASSINATE HIM.
NOW, THANKS TO YOU, THE REBELLION'S EFFORT AND ITS CHANCE ARE WASTED.
Oh.
Uh... oops.

WE'RE TRULY SORRY. IT WAS CERTAINLY NOT OUR INTENT TO CAUSE YOU ANY DIFFICULTY.
WE CAME TO ANKHARA SEARCHING FOR SOMETHING...

...THE SECOND FRAGMENT OF AYDEN'S ARROW.
THIS IS THE FIRST.
I PLAN TO GATHER THE FRAGMENTS AND BRING ABOUT MORDATH'S DESTRUCTION.

I HAVE AYDEN'S BOW AT MY BACK.
AYDEN'S BOW? TRULY?
YOU SET AN AMBITIOUS QUEST FOR YOURSELF, ARWYN OF MIDDELYN.
WE WOULD HELP YOU IF WE COULD, BUT THE FRAGMENT OF ANKHARA HAS BEEN LOST TO MY PEOPLE FOR GENERATIONS.
AND I MUST TELL YOU THAT FINDING IT IS NOT A PRIORITY, GIVEN OUR CURRENT SITUATION.

SO...TIYE? THAT'S YOUR NAME?
RAHM IS MY HUSBAND.
AND YOU MUST BE VERY HAPPY TOGETHER.
FORGET I ASKED, OKAY?

THERE'S NOTHING MORE TO BE SALVAGED HERE. COME WITH US, OR YOU SURELY DOOM YOURSELVES.
WE NEED TO BE GONE.

GONE?!

WHAT DO YOU MEAN, *THEY'RE GONE?!*
JUST... GONE, GOVERNOR KOHT.
ALL THE HAREM WOMEN, WITHOUT A TRACE. THE ONLY THING LEFT BEHIND WAS THEIR *CHAINS.*
AND THE GUARDS YOU'D SENT TO *BRING* THEM HAD BEEN SLAUGHTERED.

FIRES OF THE MASTER, WHY AM I SURROUNDED BY FOOLS AND INCOMPETENTS?!
GATHER MORE OF THE POPULATION FOR PUBLIC EXECUTIONS.
THESE DAMNED ANKHARANS WILL LEARN THEIR PLACE EVEN IF I HAVE TO DROWN THEM IN THEIR OWN BLOOD.
WNF!

GOVERNOR KOHT...
...YOU LIKELY HAVE A MORE PRESSING MATTER AT HAND.
WHO ARE YOU?
LORD MORDATH SENDING ANOTHER OF HIS LAP DOGS TO SNIFF AROUND AND JUDGE MY PROGRESS IN PUTTING DOWN THIS DAMNABLE REBELLION?
I AM SENT BY LORD MORDATH...
...BUT I COULD CARE LESS ABOUT YOUR REBELLION.

I AM CAPTAIN BOHR OF MORDATH'S GUARD. I COME FROM OUR LORD'S FORTRESS IN MIDDELYN...
...OR WHAT PRESENTLY REMAINS OF IT...
...IN SEARCH OF TWO HUMANS AND A DOG TRAVELING SOUTH. ONE, A FEMALE ARCHER, POSES A THREAT.

TWO HUMANS AND A DOG? AND THIS REQUIRES MORE THAN A DOZEN MEN?
PERHAPS MATTERS IN MIDDELYN ARE WORSE THAN I'D IMAGINED.

WE HAVE A THING IN COMMON, YOU AND I.
I COULD CARE LESS ABOUT YOUR QUARRY.
GO ABOUT YOUR BUSINESS. I HAVE OTHER CONCERNS.
MY PREDECESSOR WAS A FOOL AND LET THIS REBELLION TAKE ROOT WHILE HE GREW FAT SURROUNDED BY LUXURIES.

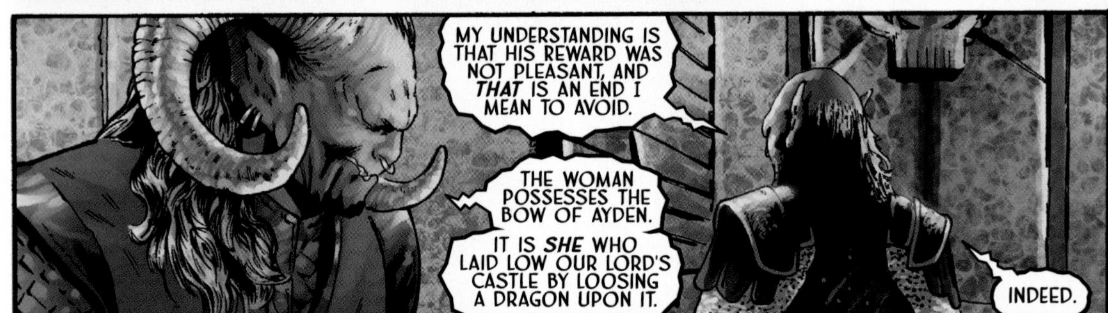
MY UNDERSTANDING IS THAT HIS REWARD WAS NOT PLEASANT, AND *THAT* IS AN END I MEAN TO AVOID.
THE WOMAN POSSESSES THE BOW OF AYDEN.
IT IS *SHE* WHO LAID LOW OUR LORD'S CASTLE BY LOOSING A DRAGON UPON IT.
INDEED.

I OVERHEARD YOUR DISCUSSION OF WHAT TRANSPIRED IN YOUR HAREM. IT IS NOT INCONCEIVABLE THAT THE INCIDENT AND MY QUARRY ARE RELATED.
THESE HUMANS HAVE PROVEN THEMSELVES SURPRISINGLY CAPABLE. THEY'VE SLIPPED AWAY FROM ME TWICE ALREADY.
IT WILL *NOT* HAPPEN AGAIN.
IT WOULD BE *ILL LUCK* FOR BOTH OF US IF THE HUMANS ARE ALREADY WITHIN THE CITY AND HAVE SOMEHOW FALLEN IN WITH THESE REBELS OF YOURS.
BUT IF WE POOLED OUR RESOURCES, PERHAPS WE COULD SOLVE MY PROBLEM *AND* YOURS.
YOU SAID IT WAS CAPTAIN *BOHR,* YES?
VERY WELL, CAPTAIN...

...TELL ME MORE.

I'M NOT SURE I *LIKE* THIS, GARETH...

...WE DON'T EVEN KNOW WHERE THEY'RE *TAKING* US.
AND I DOUBT THIS IS GOING TO HELP US FIND THE *FRAGMENT*. THE ANKHARANS AREN'T EXACTLY THE FRIENDLIEST PEOPLE I'VE EVER MET.
A LOT OF PEOPLE WOULD SAY THE SAME ABOUT *YOU*, ARWYN. YOU DON'T TEND TO BE THE *TRUSTING* TYPE, DO YOU?
NO.
NOT ANYMORE.
WELL, SINCE I DON'T THINK WE HAVE A GREAT DEAL OF CHOICE AT THIS POINT, WE MIGHT AS WELL—

WE'RE HERE.

AYDEN'S *EYES*...

THIS IS THE TEMPLE OF AMUN-SET.
ONCE IT WAS MY PEOPLE'S MOST HOLY, MOST SECRET PLACE. NOW IT IS HOME TO THOSE OF US WHO RESIST OUR OCCUPIERS.

THIS IS WHAT THE PEOPLE OF THE SUN ARE REDUCED TO.

WE, WHO ARE MEANT TO SOAR THE SKIES AND FEEL THE WIND'S CARESSES, NOW HIDE IN THE SHADOWS OF OUR OWN CITY.
WHEN THE TROLLS MARCHED UPON US WE HELD THEM OUTSIDE OUR WALLS FOR MONTHS.
WE SLEW THEM BY THE THOUSANDS, YET ALWAYS THERE WERE MORE TO TAKE THE PLACES OF THOSE THAT FELL.

THEN MORDATH HIMSELF CAME.

HIS POWER WE COULD NOT WITHSTAND.
THERE WERE THOSE WHO SAID WE SHOULD BURN WITHIN OUR AERIES AND PERISH AS A PEOPLE RATHER THAN AGAIN SUBMIT TO HIS IRON RULE.
BUT I WAS NOT AMONG THEM.
I AM THE DAWN WARRIOR.

FOR AS LONG AS THE PEOPLE OF THE SUN HAVE EXISTED...

"...THERE HAS BEEN A DAWN WARRIOR CHARGED WITH THEIR PROTECTION. IN EACH GENERATION *ONE* IS CHOSEN TO BEAR THE MANTLE...
"...AND I AM THE LATEST OF THAT UNBROKEN LINE. WE ARE TO *LEAD* IN TIMES OF WAR, AND BE VIGILANT IN TIMES OF PEACE.
"IT IS THE DAWN WARRIOR'S DUTY TO PRESERVE OUR RACE, OUR HERITAGE, ALL THAT WE ARE.
"TO THAT END WE ARE GRANTED THE MOST *POWERFUL* OF OUR ANTIQUITIES TO WIELD...
"...THE ***DAWN SWORD.***
"FORGED MILLENNIA AGO, IT HAS BEEN THE BANE OF OUR ENEMIES, A WEAPON TO HARNESS THE MIGHT OF THE SUN ITSELF.
"AND NOW IT IS *LOST* TO US.
"THE DAWN SWORD IS KEPT IN A SECRET SHRINE HIDDEN DEEP WITHIN OUR CATACOMBS IN THE CLIFFS.
"BUT THE ROUTES TO IT WERE COLLAPSED BY TROLLS SEEKING TREASURE TO SATE THEIR LUST FOR GOLD."

I AM THE DAWN WARRIOR...
...AND I HAVE FAILED IN MY DUTY.
THOSE OF MY PEOPLE WHO HAVE NOT FLED HERE, INTO THE DARKNESS, ARE LITTLE BETTER THAN SLAVES TO THESE TROLL OVERLORDS.
IT IS THE SAME IN THE OTHER CITIES OF OUR LAND.
BUT I WILL LEAD THEM FROM THE SHADOWS. I WILL FIND A WAY TO THE DAWN SWORD...
...AND THEN WE WILL TAKE BACK THIS CITY AND DESTROY THE BEASTS WHO FOUL IT.
ONCE WE HAVE DONE SO WE WILL RETAKE OUR SISTER CITIES...
...UNTIL ALL ANKHARA AGAIN BELONGS TO HER PEOPLE.
WE ARE A PROUD RACE. WE DO NOT EASILY ASK FOR HELP...
...BUT I ASK IT OF YOU NOW. THE BOW OF AYDEN WOULD BE A POWERFUL BOON TO OUR CAUSE.
SET ASIDE YOUR QUEST, AT LEAST FOR A TIME...

...AND HELP SPARE MY PEOPLE THE FATE AWAITING THEM.

ARWYN?
ARWYN?

I'LL...
...uh...
...I'LL GO SEE WHAT THAT'S ABOUT.

ARWYN?
HEY, WHAT'S GOING ON?
ARE YOU ALL RIGHT?

NO.
NO, I HAVEN'T BEEN *ALL RIGHT* IN A WHILE.

BUT...
...WELL, WHERE'S *THIS* COMING FROM? YOU'RE USUALLY SO...
...*HARDENED.*
THAT'S REALLY HOW YOU SEE ME?
I'D ALMOST THINK YOU'D LOST *BOTH* EYES, GARETH.
DON'T YOU UNDERSTAND? IT'S NOT THAT I *DON'T* FEEL...
...IT'S THAT I'M AFRAID IF I ALLOW MYSELF TO *SHOW* IT, IT MIGHT *OVERWHELM* ME.
I LOOK AT THOSE PEOPLE OUT THERE, THOSE *CHILDREN,* AND I SEE THE THINGS I'VE ALREADY LOST.
MY CITY, MY HUSBAND...
...MY DAUGHTER.
NOBODY SPARED GERRINDOR *ITS* FATE. I LOOK AT THOSE PEOPLE AND I WONDER WHAT MIGHT'VE HAPPENED IF SOMEONE...
...IF SOMEONE HAD BEEN ABLE TO...
...JUST...
...*NEVER MIND.*
IT DOESN'T MATTER.

OF COURSE IT MATTERS.
ARWYN, I KNOW WHAT YOU'VE SUFFERED, AND I KNOW YOU'VE CHOSEN TO UNDERTAKE THIS QUEST. NOW THERE'S ANOTHER CHOICE IN FRONT OF YOU.
GATHERING THE FIVE FRAGMENTS, HELPING THE ANKHARANS, EVEN WALKING AWAY FROM THE WHOLE THING.

THIS REBELLION ISN'T OUR BATTLE. AT BEST IT'LL SLOW US DOWN, AT WORST I SUPPOSE IT MIGHT GET US KILLED.
WE CAN SAY NO, TRY TO FIND THE FRAGMENT ON OUR OWN, AND THEN CONTINUE SOUTH INTO OUDUBAI.
WE CAN STAY AND FIGHT.
OR WE CAN FORGET ALL OF IT.

BUT IT IS YOUR CHOICE. AND I'LL STAND BY WHATEVER YOU DECIDE.
I'LL...DO WHATEVER YOU WANT ME TO DO, ARWYN.

ARWYN?
SO WHAT ARE WE DOING?

THEY ARE NOT OF OUR PEOPLE, RAHM. YOU EXPECT TOO MUCH OF THEM.
WHAT *CHOICE* HAVE WE, ELDER? IF OUR CIVILIZATION IS NOT TO PASS FROM THE FACE OF THE WORLD—
ALL RIGHT...

...WHERE DO WE *START?*
And that's how we joined the Ankharan rebellion.
Of course, at that point I didn't know it would get me executed.

LAND
LEISTEN
JP3

mmnnf
Whuh?
Shhh...

...LET'S NOT BE *LOUD*.
WE DON'T WANT TO WAKE THE OTHERS.
ARWYN? Uh...
...*ARWYN?*

YES, ARWYN.
WHY, WERE YOU EXPECTING SOMEONE ELSE?
WELL...NO. TRUTHFULLY, I WASN'T EXPECTING... ANYONE.
I MEAN, I THOUGHT YOU AND I WERE SUPPOSED TO BE, YOU KNOW, PLATONIC.
NOT THAT I'M COMPLAINING BUT...
...WHAT ARE YOU DOING?
Oh, I THINK IT'S PRETTY OBVIOUS WHAT I'M DOING, DON'T YOU?
IT'S TIME WE STOPPED ACTING LIKE THERE'S NOTHING GOING ON BETWEEN US.
I FEEL IT. I KNOW YOU DO, TOO...
...SO WHY DON'T WE FINALLY LET IT HAPPEN, GARETH?

GARETH.
GARETH, WAKE UP.
ARE YOU ALL RIGHT? YOU LOOK A LITTLE... STARTLED.
Uh... YEAH, I WAS JUST... um...
...DREAMING.
ABOUT THE SECOND FRAGMENT?
NO.
NOT THAT KIND OF DREAM.
WHAT'S GOING ON?
RAHM'S GATHERING EVERYONE.
LET'S GO.
SURE THING. I'LL BE RIGHT THERE. JUST...
...GIVE ME A MINUTE.

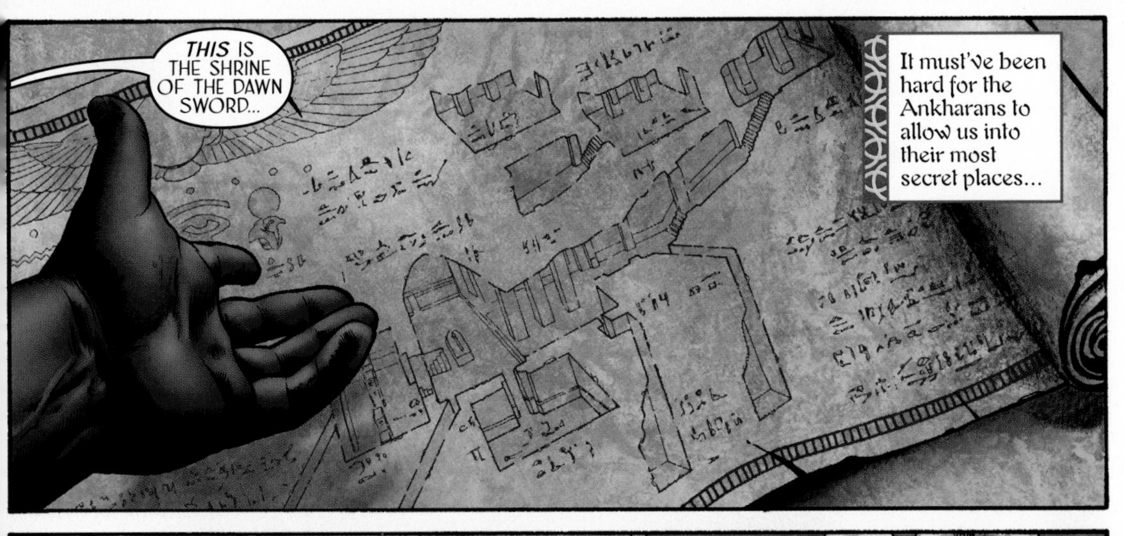
It must've been hard for the Ankharans to allow us into their most secret places...
THIS IS THE SHRINE OF THE DAWN SWORD...

...much less ask for help from a couple of mud-walkers.
That's their name for us, you know.
...BUT IT IS UNREACHABLE. WE HAVE SEARCHED FOR AN ALTERNATE ACCESS TO THE SHRINE, BUT ONE HAS YET TO BE FOUND.
WHEN MORDATH'S TROLLS TOOK THE CITY, THEY SET ABOUT SEARCHING FOR RICHES TO LOOT.
THEIR GREED FOR GOLD OVERCAME THEIR FEAR OF OUR HONORED DEAD. THE TROLLS GAINED ENTRANCE TO SOME OF OUR PASSAGEWAYS...
...BUT THE FOOLS CAUSED COLLAPSES. THE WAY TO THE SHRINE IS NOW UNPASSABLE.

SO...
...WHAT'D I MISS?

WE MUST FIND ANOTHER ROUTE INTO THE SHRINE VIA PASSAGEWAYS ABANDONED LONG AGO. I MUST TAKE UP THE DAWN SWORD.
WE WHO HAVE CHOSEN TO RESIST THE TROLLS ARE TOO FEW. BUT THE SWORD'S POWER COULD HELP DRIVE OUT OUR OCCUPIERS AND RALLY THE PEOPLE.
OTHERWISE...
They're famously aloof, the Ankharans.
And that's the nice way to put it.
In the time I'd spent among them previously, I was never viewed as anything but an inferior.
...OTHERWISE I WILL HAVE FAILED IN MY SACRED DUTY AS DAWN WARRIOR.
AS MY PEOPLE'S PROTECTOR.
They keep to themselves, cloistered in their cities carved from cliffs.
And who can blame them, really?
I TOLD RAHM WE'D HELP WITH THE SEARCH.
MAKES SENSE.
I'M SURE A GUY WITH ONE EYE AND AN ARCHER WITH ONE ARM WILL BE A BIG HELP IN LOOKING FOR—
Shush.
OOF!

ALL RIGHT, SO WHAT ARE WE LOOKING AT HERE?
MOST OF THE LOWER PASSAGES WERE NEVER MAPPED BEFORE THEY WERE ABANDONED, BUT THEY ARE OUR ONLY HOPE OF REACHING THE SHRINE.
WE'LL SPLIT INTO SEARCH PARTIES...

...TIYE LEADING ONE GROUP...
...HAMET ANOTHER...

...WHILE THE TWO OF *YOU* WILL GO WITH ME.
ARCHER, I KNOW YOU CAME TO MY LAND SEEKING YOUR OWN PRIZE, I WOULD AID YOU IF I COULD...
Why consort with those of us who are forever chained to the mundane ground...
...when they can soar high above the skin of the world?

...BUT AYDEN'S FRAGMENT HAS BEEN LOST SINCE BEFORE THE TIME OF MY FATHER'S FATHER.
MY QUEST WILL HAVE TO WAIT.
MAYBE BY HELPING *YOU* WE CAN HELP OURSELVES.
I know I can think of at least one instance when flying would've come in handy.
But we'll get to that part in a bit.

NO ONE HAS WALKED THE LOWER PASSAGES IN A GENERATION. WE SEALED THESE CORRIDORS WHEN WE NO LONGER HAD NEED OF THEM...
...AND THEY HAVEN'T BEEN OPENED SINCE.
Augh.
YOU DON'T SAY.
FROM THE SMELL OF IT, I'D SAY THE AIR'S NOT THE ONLY THING THAT'S DEAD IN THERE.
FOLLOW CLOSELY...
...THIS WOULD NOT BE A WISE PLACE TO LOSE YOUR WAY.
SO WHY DRAG THE BOW ALONG, ARWYN? IT'S NOT LIKE YOU'RE IN ANY SHAPE TO USE IT.
IS AYDEN'S BOW THE SORT OF THING YOU'D LEAVE LYING AROUND?
THIS COMES WITH ME WHEREVER I GO...
...WHETHER I CAN ACTUALLY PULL IT OR NOT.

HOW'S THE ARM *FEEL?*
YOU HAVE TO BE ANXIOUS TO GET RID OF THAT SLING.
MORE THAN ANXIOUS. THERE'S REALLY NO *PAIN* ANYMORE...

...BUT I'D RATHER NOT RISK DOING MORE DAMAGE IF IT'S NOT COMPLETELY HEALED.
MAYBE ANOTHER WEEK AND—

WAIT...
...WHAT'S...

ARWYN!

I'VE GOT YOU.
HANG ON...
HNF
...HANG ON AND I'LL PULL YOU BACK UP.
I NEED TO GET A BETTER GRIP...
GARETH, I'M SLIPPING. I'M...
ARWYN!
FOR A GUY WITH WINGS IT TOOK YOU LONG ENOUGH TO GET BACK HERE, RAHM!
WHERE WOULD THIS COLLAPSE GO? HOW DO WE REACH IT?
I TOLD YOU, THESE PASSAGES WERE NEVER MAPPED.
I DON'T KNOW WHERE SHE IS. AND EVEN IF I DID...

"...I DON'T KNOW HOW WE'D REACH HER."
mmmnn...

...NO.
NO, NO, NO...
...DON'T YOU *DARE* GO OUT.

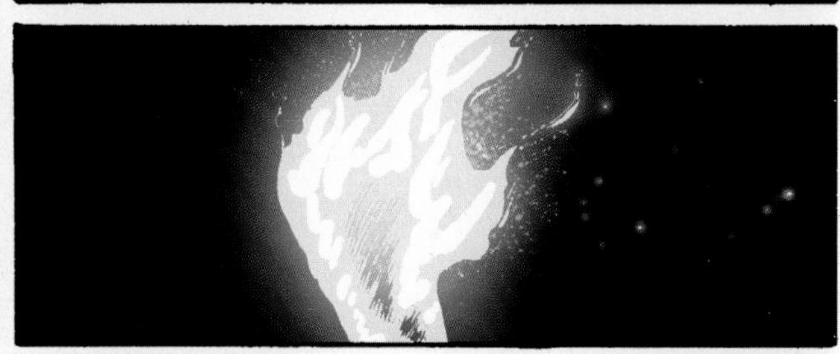

THAT'S BETTER.
AT LEAST I CAN *SEE* WHERE I AM...

...WHEREVER THAT IS.
What happened between us?
That's really what you want to know, not how arrogant the Ankharans were or how they buried their dead.
Hard not to fall in love with her at least a little, isn't it?

Yes, she was beautiful, that much is obvious. Didn't need two eyes to see that.
But there was so much more.
THE DAWN SWORD.
IT *MUST* BE.
Her strength. Her sense of honor.
And that aura of sadness so palpable you immediately wanted to fix it.
Even though Arwyn was about the last person who needed it...

...you naturally
wanted to protect her.

As far as what she thought of me at that point...
...I don't know.
HRRRR

Most other women knew within a day whether they wanted to kiss me or slap me.

Sometimes both.
But with Arwyn...

...Arwyn was different.

She'd lost her husband and her daughter, everything that meant anything to her.
HWF!

I knew that.

And I also knew a relationship, any kind of relationship, was the last thing on her mind.
But there also was an inevitability that came from being together all the time, depending upon each other for survival.
I GUESS NOW'S WHEN WE FIND OUT...

...IF I'M UP TO DOING THIS.

It would almost be surprising if something didn't happen.
THAT'S RIGHT...

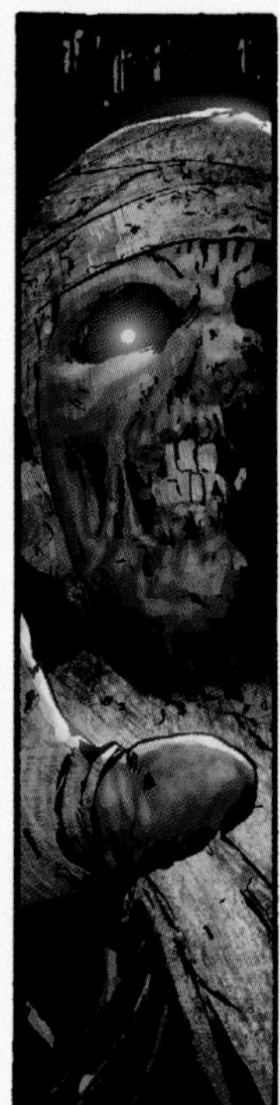

...KEEP COMING.
Assuming we both stayed alive long enough.

ARWYN?

ARWYN!
I WASN'T SURE WE WERE EVER GOING TO SEE YOU AGAIN. YOU STILL IN ONE PIECE?
HROOF

I'M...FINE, GIVEN THE CIRCUMSTANCES.
SO'S MY ARM, APPARENTLY.
HOW DID YOU GET HERE, GARETH?
YOU HAVE YOUR DOG TO THANK.

AS SOON AS YOU DISAPPEARED KREEG SET OFF AT A RUN. HE LED US THROUGH SOME PRETTY TIGHT PLACES, BUT HERE WE ARE.
EITHER HE FOLLOWED HIS NOSE OR YOU TWO HAVE SOME SPOOKY CONNECTION I DON'T WANT TO CONTEMPLATE.
GOOD BOY.
I'M GLAD TO SEE YOU, TOO.

HERE, YOU DROPPED THIS.
OR IT DROPPED YOU.
THANKS.

CARE TO EXPLAIN WHAT HAPPENED HERE?
I WOULD IF I COULD. WHEN I TRIED TO PICK UP THE SWORD THAT...
...THING...
...CAME AFTER ME. THERE'S NO WAY IT COULD'VE BEEN ALIVE, BUT...

BUT IT WAS. I TOLD YOU THE ANKHARANS WERE A PRETTY MYSTERIOUS BUNCH.
MAYBE A GUARDIAN MEANT TO KEEP THE SWORD OUT OF THE HANDS OF INFIDELS LIKE US?
I DON'T KNOW...

"...BUT AT LEAST HE'S FOUND WHAT HE'S LOOKING FOR."

NOW I WILL SET MY PEOPLE *FREE*.

YOU KNOW...
...I THINK I'VE GOT AN IDEA.

AAAGH!

WHY DO YOU RESIST ME?
YOU SAW WHAT HAPPENED TO YOUR FELLOWS. YOU KNOW WHAT WILL HAPPEN TO YOU.
SOMEONE WILL TELL ME. IF NOT YOU, THEN THE NEXT, OR THE ONE AFTER.
SPARE YOURSELF THIS PAIN. SPARE YOURSELF THIS FATE.
nnhh

TELL ME.
TELL ME WHERE THE REBELS ARE HIDING!
NOTHING, KOHT. I TELL YOU NOTHING.
THAT SECRET I TAKE TO MY GRAVE.

YES. YOU DO.
GET RID OF HIM...

...AND BRING ME ANOTHER.

It seemed like a good idea at the time.
Really it did.
NOW HAUL AWAY...

...AND PULL FOR ALL YOU'RE WORTH, YOU DOGS!
PULL!

I WANT THIS DAMNED UGLY THING ON THE GROUND AND IN PIECES...
...AND I WANT THOSE GEMSTONE EYES!
BLASPHEMER!
YOU DEFACE EVEN OUR GODS!
STILL YOUR TONGUE UNLESS YOU WANT TO LOSE IT, OLD MAN!
ALL OF YOU ANKHARANS LIVE ONLY AT THE MERCY OF OUR LORD MORDATH, AND THEN ONLY IF YOU KEEP YOUR PLACE.
IF IT WAS UP TO ME, I'D HAVE EVERY LAST ONE OF YOU THROWN FROM THE CLIFFS.
MAYBE YOU'D PREFER TO KEEP YOUR TONGUE AND HAVE YOUR EYES SCOOPED FROM YOUR SKULL.
BETTER THAT THAN WATCH THE EYES OF YOUR GOD PRIED FROM THEIR SOCKETS, hm? I CAN MAKE THAT—
HRRK!

NICE SHOT.
THANKS.

THE HUMANS!
THE ONES GOVERNOR KOHT WANTS!

COME AND GET US.

YOU KNOW, I THINK WE'VE GOT THEIR *ATTENTION*.
TAKE THEM!
I THINK YOU MIGHT HAVE A POINT.
UGF!
GETTING A LITTLE *CROWDED* HERE, ARWYN...
...MIGHT BE A PRUDENT TIME TO *RELOCATE*.

HWNF!
AT THIS POINT...
...I'M WILLING TO CONCEDE MAYBE THIS WASN'T SUCH A GREAT PLAN AFTER ALL.

LET'S NOT FORGET...
HRG!
...WHOSE IDEA IT WAS.

WELL, LET'S NOT FORGET WHO AGREED TO IT!
"TRUST ME," YOU SAID.

HK!
YEAH, I DID SAY THAT.

YOU HAVE TO ADMIT...
...THAT WHOLE "GET THE TROLLS TO CHASE US" PART WORKS FINE.
WE NEVER SEEM TO HAVE A PROBLEM WITH THAT PART.

TAKE THEM ALIVE!
THE GOVERNOR WANTS THEM ALIVE!

THAT'S ENCOURAGING.
WE'RE RUNNING OUT OF ROOM IN A HURRY HERE, ARWYN.
JUST HOPE THEY DON'T GET CARRIED AWAY.

NO WONDER THESE PEOPLE LIKE HAVING WINGS SO MUCH.
HRK!
THIS HAD BETTER *WORK,* GARETH!
COME ON, WHAT COULD GO WRONG?

TELL US...
...YOU WILL TELL US WHAT WE WANT TO KNOW!
ANSWER ME, HUMAN!
WHERE...
...WHERE AM I?
SOMEPLACE YOU DON'T WANT TO BE.
I AM KOHT. I AM GOVERNOR HERE, BY THE WILL OF OUR LORD MORDATH.
WHERE'S GARETH?
YOU STILL HAVEN'T SAID PLEASE YET.
OR DID I MISS THAT?

QUITE NEAR...
...AND YET FAR BEYOND YOUR ABILITY TO HELP HIM.
HOW COME SHE GETS A CHAIR?
I DON'T GET A CHAIR.

LET HIM GO.

THAT WILL NOT HAPPEN.
WE HAVE NEVER PROPERLY MET. I AM BOHR.
MORDATH HIMSELF TASKED ME WITH YOUR CAPTURE. I MUST ADMIT YOU'VE DONE ADMIRABLY.
YOU'VE MANAGED TO SLIP AWAY FROM ME ON MORE THAN ONE OCCASION.
BUT THE CHASE HAS COME TO AN END.
WHAT ARE YOU PLANNING TO DO WITH US?

YOUR FATES ARE NO LONGER INTERTWINED.
MORDATH DESIRES YOU ALIVE, BOHR WILL DELIVER YOU TO HIM.
THIS OTHER...

...HE WILL BE USEFUL TO ME WHEN HIS TONGUE IS PROPERLY LOOSENED.
YOU BOTH HAVE BEEN WITH THE REBELLION. I WOULD KNOW WHERE THE REBELS HIDE.
ONCE I KNOW THAT, I WILL CRUSH THIS REBELLION AS IF IT HAD NEVER EXISTED.
GARETH, NO!
YOU CAN'T TELL THEM!
I'M NOT TELLING THESE GREEN-SKINS A DAMNED THING!
BE SILENT.
WHFF!
YOUR FRIEND'S THRESHOLD FOR PAIN HAS BEEN IMPRESSIVE.
HE'S BEEN QUITE UNWILLING TO TALK, SAVE TO GIVE MY MEN ANY NUMBER OF SUGGESTIONS CONCERNING THEIR PARENTAGE AS WELL AS CERTAIN BODILY ORIFICES.
BUT WHILE HIS WILLPOWER MAY BE ADMIRABLE...
...MY DUTY HERE IS TO PUT DOWN THIS REBELLION.
AND I WILL USE ANY MEANS NECESSARY TO DO SO.

LISTEN, ARE WE FINALLY GONNA GET SERIOUS ABOUT THIS? BECAUSE I'VE BEEN TORTURED BY SOME OF THE BEST, AND TO BE HONEST WITH YOU...
...THESE GUYS OF YOURS ARE AMATEURS. NOT MUCH STYLE.
THEN I'LL TRY NOT TO DISAPPOINT YOU. I HAVE HAD...
...SOME EXPERIENCE...
...IN THIS SORT OF THING.
LET US UNDERSTAND SOMETHING. YOU ARE GOING TO DIE. I PROMISE YOU THAT WITH ABSOLUTE CERTAINTY.
YOU ARE GOING TO DIE AND YOU ARE GOING TO TELL ME WHAT I WANT TO KNOW. YOU HAVE NO CHOICE IN THIS.
THE ONLY CHOICE YOU HAVE IS HOW MUCH YOU SUFFER BETWEEN NOW AND WHEN I GRANT YOU THAT RELEASE.
THAT CHOICE IS YOURS.
TELL ME WHAT I WISH TO KNOW, AND YOUR DEATH WILL BE QUICK.
DEFY ME, AND IT WILL SEEM ENDLESS.
ARE YOU DONE TALKING, SHORTY? BECAUSE I'M READY WHEN YOU—
AARRR!
NOW.
TELL ME OF THE REBELS. WHERE IS THEIR LAIR?
CAN'T REMEMBER.

Oh, I THINK YOU WILL.
GYAAH!

GHH
GHH
GET BENT.

VERY WELL. I CAN BE PATIENT...

...CAN YOU?

AAAHG!

STOP!
STOP, THAT'S ENOUGH!
YOU CANNOT HELP HIM...

...ONLY HE CAN HELP HIMSELF NOW.
IS THIS PERHAPS HOW YOU LOST YOUR OTHER EYE?
CARD GAME.
SEWING ACCIDENT.
RUNNING WITH SCISSORS.

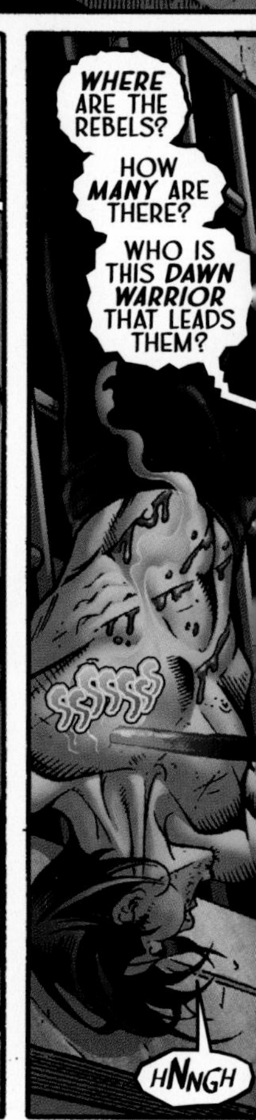
WHERE ARE THE REBELS?
HOW MANY ARE THERE?
WHO IS THIS DAWN WARRIOR THAT LEADS THEM?
SSSSS
HNNGH

BURIAL CHAMBER...
WHAT?
...BURIAL CHAMBER...
...DEEP IN THE CATACOMBS...
...I CAN DRAW YOU A MAP.
THERE'S LESS THAN A HUNDRED OF THEM, INCLUDING WOMEN AND CHILDREN.
THE REBELS... THOUGHT YOU'D BE AFRAID TO LOOK THERE, SO THEY'VE BEEN USING IT AS THEIR HIDING PLACE.
IT'S WHERE THEY'VE BEEN KEEPING THEIR *TREASURE* AS WELL, PILES OF GOLD AND JEWELS.
I SWEAR, THAT'S EVERYTHING I KNOW...

Oh, GARETH...

YOU GOT WHAT YOU WANTED. PLEASE, I'M NO THREAT TO MORDATH...
...AT LEAST LET *ME* GO.

HOW CONVENIENTLY ***DISPOSABLE*** YOUR LOYALTY IS.
NO, I DON'T ***THINK*** SO.
I PROMISED YOU YOU'D DIE, AND SO YOU SHALL. I HAVE A ***SPECIAL*** END IN MIND FOR YOU.

It was hard for those words to even come out of my mouth.

I'd no more leave Arwyn to Mordath's mercies than I could fly.
WHMP

But the trolls didn't know that, so it was worth a try.
KRAKT

I thought if I could get away...
GOVERNOR KOHT SAID THIS IS WHERE THE REBELS WOULD BE...

...I might be able to come back and free Arwyn before Bohr took her.
Shame it didn't turn out that way.
...BUT THEY'RE NOT HERE.
Bohr was a wild card. We'd assumed he was still following us, but we hadn't guessed he was already in Ankhara.
Everything else had gone as we'd expected...

...including being captured and tortured.
THIS IS JUST AN EMPTY TOMB.

NOT *EMPTY.*
IT'S TRUE, THERE *IS* TREASURE HERE.
I didn't mind taking the punishment.
Much.

KEEP YOUR WITS ABOUT YOU, DAMN YOU!
YOU'RE NOT HERE TO LINE YOUR POCKETS!

And I really had been tortured by some of the best.
But it had to be convincing.
Feh.
DISGUSTING WAY TO BURY YOUR DEAD.

HRRK!
How else were we going to lead the fools into a trap?

That's really where the Ankharan rebellion took root.
We used the trolls' greed against them. We used their superstitions.
Their utter shock at having "the dead" rise up against them gave us the advantage of surprise.
It gave us a chance.
I would've given a lot to see their faces...

...but unfortunately I was otherwise occupied.
YOU SHARE THE DEATH OF OTHER REBELS...
...THOUGH YOU DON'T NEED YOUR WINGS CLIPPED.
IT TAKES QUITE SOME TIME TO STRIKE BOTTOM.
I'LL BET.
I OWE YOU MY THANKS. I'M SURE MY TROOPS ARE BUTCHERING THE REBELS EVEN NOW.
Oh, I'M SURE THERE'S BLOOD BEING SPILLED.
I'LL JOIN MY MEN SHORTLY. BUT I WANTED TO SEE TO YOUR PUNISHMENT PERSONALLY.
NICE TO KNOW YOU CARE.
IT'S NOT SUPPOSED TO BE LIKE THIS!

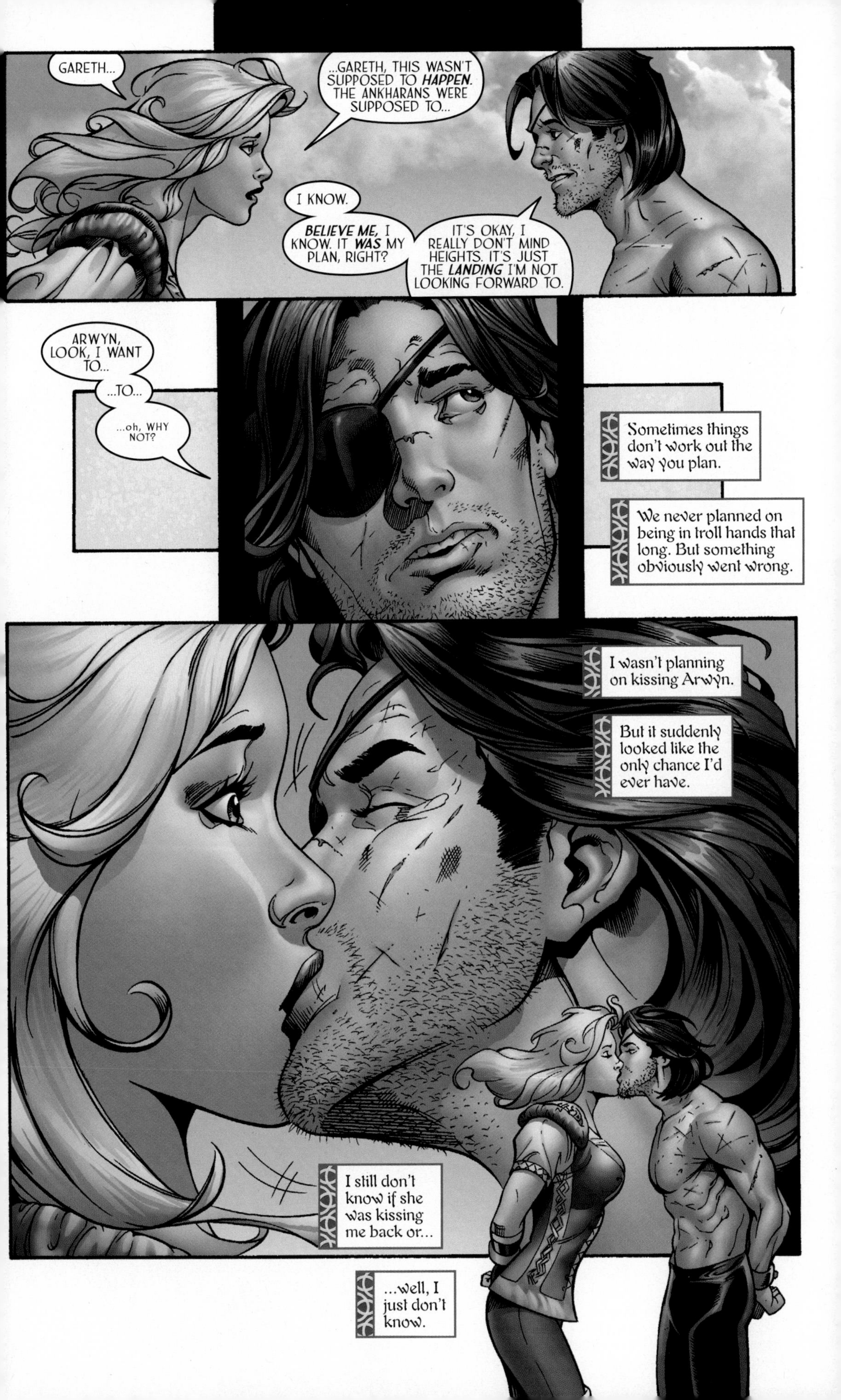
GARETH...
...GARETH, THIS WASN'T SUPPOSED TO HAPPEN. THE ANKHARANS WERE SUPPOSED TO...
I KNOW.
BELIEVE ME, I KNOW. IT WAS MY PLAN, RIGHT?
IT'S OKAY, I REALLY DON'T MIND HEIGHTS. IT'S JUST THE LANDING I'M NOT LOOKING FORWARD TO.
ARWYN, LOOK, I WANT TO...
...TO...
...oh, WHY NOT?
Sometimes things don't work out the way you plan.
We never planned on being in troll hands that long. But something obviously went wrong.
I wasn't planning on kissing Arwyn.
But it suddenly looked like the only chance I'd ever have.
I still don't know if she was kissing me back or...
...well, I just don't know.

GARETH?
HOW TOUCHING...
...NOW GET RID OF HIM.
I can think of worse ways to go than pitched off a cliff. Not many, but a few.
The thing is, I didn't really have any regrets. At least my life had been worthy of a story or two.
But I do wish I'd been around to see how this particular one ended.

GARETH!

LET GO OF ME!
GARETH!

GARETH?

PULL HER BACK FROM THE EDGE.
I DON'T WANT HER *PITCHING HERSELF OFF* AFTER HER BOYFRIEND...

YOU FILTH! IT WASN'T SUPPOSED TO BE LIKE THIS!
HE TOLD YOU WHAT YOU WANTED TO KNOW AND YOU KILLED HIM ANYWAY!
...SHE'S TOO VALUABLE ALIVE.
GET HER READY. WE'RE LEAVING.

UNTRUE.
CAPTAIN BOHR HAD NOTHING TO DO WITH YOUR COMPANION'S DEATH.
I ORDERED HIM KILLED AFTER HE REVEALED THE WHEREABOUTS OF THE REBELS. HE WAS NO LONGER OF USE TO ME.

I'LL SEE YOU DEAD, KOHT. I SWEAR TO YOU I WILL.
I FIND THAT UNLIKELY.

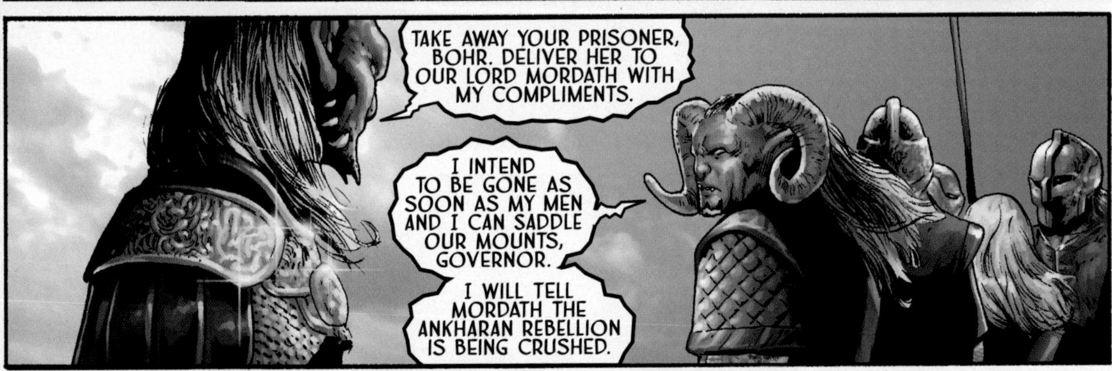
TAKE AWAY YOUR PRISONER, BOHR. DELIVER HER TO OUR LORD MORDATH WITH MY COMPLIMENTS.
I INTEND TO BE GONE AS SOON AS MY MEN AND I CAN SADDLE OUR MOUNTS, GOVERNOR.
I WILL TELL MORDATH THE ANKHARAN REBELLION IS BEING CRUSHED.

IT WILL BE CRUSHED LONG BEFORE YOU REACH MIDDELYN.
NOW THAT WE KNOW WHERE THE REBELS HAVE BEEN HIDING...

"...MY TROOPS WILL SLAUGHTER EVERY LAST ONE OF THEM."
AAGH!

HUNT THEM DOWN!
HUNT DOWN OUR OPPRESSORS AND SLAY THEM!

GHRG!
WE ARE LURED INTO A *TRAP!*
RETREAT!
RETR—

EVERY LAST ONE OF THEM.

THE TROLLS FLEE BACK TO THE STREETS IN *TERROR,* DAWN WARRIOR.
AS WE KNEW THEY WOULD.
THE PLAN SUCCEEDS.

OUR ALLIES WERE ABLE TO LEAD THE TROLLS TO US...

"...NOW WE MUST FREE *THEM* FROM THE CLUTCHES OF OUR ENEMIES."
MIND YOUR *CHARGE,* KNECHT.
SHE'D SOONER SLIT YOUR THROAT THAN LOOK AT YOU, AND SHE'S WELL ABLE TO *DO* IT GIVEN HALF A CHANCE.
NOW THAT WE FINALLY *HAVE* HER, WE CAN ILL AFFORD TO LOSE HER.
IF WE RIDE *HARD* WE CAN BE BACK AT MORDATH'S FORTRESS WITHIN A WEEK. AND WE DELIVER NOT ONLY THE *WOMAN* TO OUR MASTER...

...BUT *AYDEN'S BOW* AS WELL.
CAPTAIN, IS THIS TRULY THE—

HLLK!
THUK

ARWYN!
TIYE...

WE'RE NOT LEAVING YOU TO THEIR MERCIES.
MY BOW!
MAKE SURE MY BOW ISN'T LEFT BEHIND!
WE NEED YOU...

...AND YOUR WEAPON.

STOP THEM!
STOP THEM BEFORE THEY...

WHERE IS THE OTHER?
GARETH.
WHERE HAVE YOU BEEN?! YOU WERE SUPPOSED TO RESCUE US!
KOHT THREW GARETH FROM THE CLIFFS. WE HAVE TO GO BACK FOR HIM!
WE HAVE TO GO BACK!
...GET AWAY.

WE'RE LUCKY TO HAVE FOUND YOU AT ALL. WE MEANT TO REACH YOU SOONER, BUT WE NEVER SUSPECTED KOHT WOULD TAKE YOU TO THE CLIFFS.
NO ONE SURVIVES THAT FALL.
GARETH, MORE THAN ANYONE, KNEW THE RISKS OF PERPETRATING THIS RUSE.
NO, THERE HAS TO BE A CHANCE. HE COULD HAVE—

IF YOUR FRIEND WAS HURLED FROM THE CLIFFS, HE IS DEAD.
GOING BACK TO FIND HIS CORPSE WILL SERVE NO PURPOSE.
I'M SORRY, ARWYN.

WE HAVE TO RETURN TO THE CITY...

"...THE FINAL BATTLE HAS BEEN JOINED."
HOW CAN THIS BE?
FIGHT, YOU FOOLS!
TURN AND FIGHT!
THE DEAD RISE!
THEY TAKE THEIR VENGEANCE!
HRRG!

PEOPLE OF THE SUN!
THE DAWN WARRIOR CALLS YOU!
GHRRGLL

THE DAWN SWORD IS FOUND AND IT IS *RAISED!*

YOU HAVE CLUNG TO THE HOPE THAT A DAY OF *RETRIBUTION* WOULD COME!
A DAY OF *JUSTICE!*
THAT DAY IS *HERE!*

THE SWORD BURNS *BRIGHT,* MY PEOPLE!
RISE UP!
RISE UP AND TAKE BACK YOUR *CITY!* TAKE BACK YOUR *FREEDOM!*

WE MAKE OUR STAND.
HERE.
YES, GOVERNOR.

RAHM!
ARWYN?
WHERE IS GARETH?

DEAD.
YOU DIDN'T REACH US IN TIME.
I AM SORRY. WE DID TRY.

HRUFF
KREEG...

...I'M HAPPY TO SEE YOU TOO, BOY.
I REGRET YOUR FRIEND'S DEATH, ARWYN.
IT WAS HIS PLAN THAT ALLOWED US THIS OPPORTUNITY...

...BUT YOU'LL AT LEAST HAVE YOUR CHANCE AT REVENGE.
YES...

"...I WILL HAVE THAT."

"THE STREETS RUN RED WITH YOUR BLOOD. YOUR DEAD LITTER THE GROUND..."

"...WHILE MY PEOPLE FLY FREE. THE BATTLE IS ENDED..."

...AND OUR CITY AGAIN BELONGS TO US.
YOU ARE THE ONE?
YOU ARE THIS DAWN WARRIOR WHO LEADS THEM?
I AM.
I AM THE PROTECTOR OF MY PEOPLE. I AM THE BANE OF OUR ENEMIES.
MY MEN ARE DEAD. BUT THIS IS NOT YET OVER...

...NOT WHILE I STILL DRAW BREATH.
I WON'T BEG FOR YOUR MERCY.

I WASN'T OFFERING IT.

CHANG
GF!
GYAAH!

FINISH IT.
THIS IS MERELY A BEGINNING.

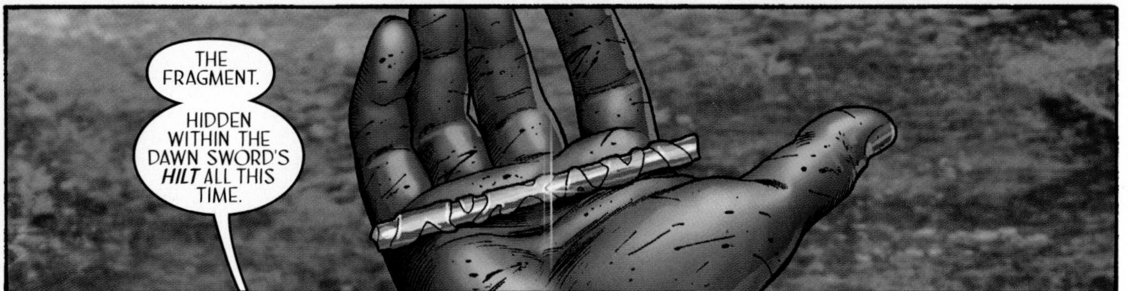
THE FRAGMENT.
HIDDEN WITHIN THE DAWN SWORD'S HILT ALL THIS TIME.

THIS IS WHAT YOU WERE SEEKING.
YES.
YOU AIDED US WHEN IT WOULD HAVE BEEN FAR EASIER FOR YOU TO MOVE ON.
IN SETTING ASIDE YOUR QUEST, YOU GAINED THE OBJECT OF YOUR QUEST.

INDEED, YOU ARE THE FAVORED OF THE GODS.
THIS IS YOURS.
BUT...
...IF AYDEN'S FRAGMENT GAVE THE DAWN SWORD ITS POWER...

NO.
THE FRAGMENT MUST HAVE BEEN PLACED WITHIN THE HILT MERELY TO SAFEGUARD IT.
THE DAWN SWORD WAS A POWERFUL WEAPON EVEN BEFORE THE FRAGMENT EXISTED.
A NEW HILT WILL BE MADE FOR THE BLADE, AND IT WILL BE AS IT ALWAYS WAS.
PLEASE...

...TAKE THE FRAGMENT.
THANK YOU.
ALL IT COST WAS GARETH'S LIFE.

I GRIEVE THAT YOUR FRIEND WAS LOST. HE HAS BEEN *AVENGED*...
...BUT I KNOW THAT DOES NOT LESSEN YOUR PAIN.
YOU *CAN* STAY WITH US, ARWYN. WE DO NOT ACCEPT OUTSIDERS EASILY, BUT YOU HAVE *EARNED* A PLACE HERE.
NOW THAT WE HAVE TAKEN OUR LAND'S CAPITAL, THE REBELLION CAN SPREAD TO OTHER CITIES IN ANKHARA. YOU WOULD BE A *BOON* TO OUR CAUSE.

I'M FLATTERED THAT YOUR PEOPLE WOULD ACCEPT ME, RAHM. BUT I *SWORE* I WOULD SEE MORDATH DESTROYED...
...AND I DO NOT BELIEVE THAT WILL HAPPEN BY SIMPLE INSURRECTION.
I MUST CONTINUE MY QUEST, NOW MORE THAN EVER. I HAVE *TWO* OF THE FIVE FRAGMENTS...
...BUT *EACH* WAS BOUGHT WITH A LIFE.

THEN CAN ONE OF MY WARRIORS *ACCOMPANY* YOU?
IT'S THE *LEAST* WE OWE YOU.
I APPRECIATE YOUR KINDNESS, RAHM...

...BUT THUS FAR THOSE WHO HAVE *HELPED* ME HAVE COME TO DIRE ENDS. I WON'T DOOM ANY *OTHERS* TO THAT FATE.
I'LL STAY IN ANKHARA ONLY LONG ENOUGH TO GATHER SUPPLIES AND FIND A MOUNT. THEN I CONTINUE SOUTH TOWARD OUDUBAI.
THIS QUEST MUST BE MINE...

"...AND MINE ALONE."

REPORT.
THE CITY IS *LOST,* MY CAPTAIN.
THE REBELS HAVE SLAIN NEARLY *ALL* OF THE OCCUPIERS, INCLUDING GOVERNOR KOHT.

I BARELY MANAGED TO ESCAPE WITH MY LIFE.
IT WAS WISE OF YOU TO KEEP OUR FORCE OUTSIDE THE WALLS. *WE* SURELY WOULD HAVE BEEN SLAUGHTERED AS WELL.
WHAT NOW? WHAT OF OUR *QUARRY?*
BOUND FOR OUDUBAI, I'M CERTAIN.

SHE'LL DEPART VIA THE CITY'S SOUTH GATE. SHE LIKELY ALREADY *HAS.*
WE'LL HAVE TO FIND A WAY AROUND. THE WOMAN WILL GAIN *DAYS* ON US...

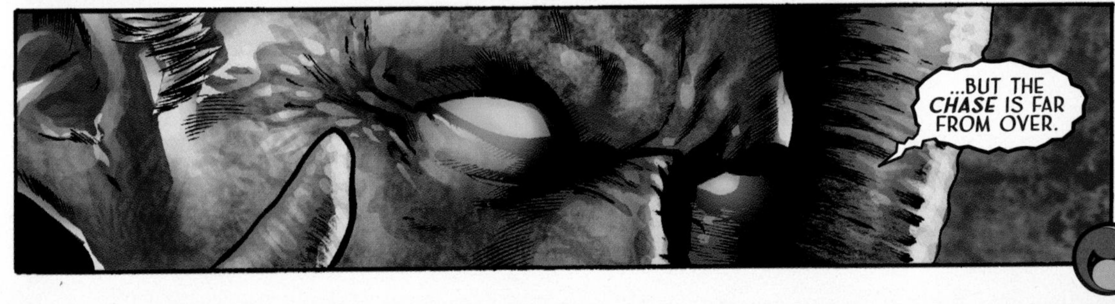
...BUT THE *CHASE* IS FAR FROM OVER.

Artist Greg Land receives a great many requests for illustrations of Arwyn, giving him the opportunity to depict the archer in finished tonal pencil renderings. Presented here are a few of those pieces, most published for the first time.

LAND

LAND

LAND

LAND

LANO